For all the kids, just like me, who love to dance – J.C.

For Sonny & Teddy – F.L.

First published in Great Britain in 2021 by Andersen Press Ltd.,
20 Vauxhall Bridge Road, London SW1V 2SA, UK.
Vijverlaan 48, 3062 HL Rotterdam, Nederland.
Text copyright © Joseph Coelho 2021. Illustration copyright © Fiona Lumbers 2021.
The rights of Joseph Coelho and Fiona Lumbers to be identified as the author and
illustrator of this work have been asserted by them in accordance with the Copyright,
Designs and Patents Act, 1988. All rights reserved. Printed and bound in China.
10 9 8 7 6 5 4 3 2 1
British Library Cataloguing in Publication Data available. ISBN 978 1 83913 056 4

Luna Loves Dance

Joseph Coelho

Andersen Press

Fiona Lumbers

Luna loves dance.
Twirling at Dad's,

leaping at Mum's.

When Luna dances
it's like the world's volume turns up,
like all colours brighten,
like sunlight sparkles behind every cloud.

Today is the day of her dance exam.

Dance shoes – check!
Dance tutu – check!
Dance bag – check!

Mum and Dad watch
as the dance teacher
shows the class

a double-tap-spin
duck-dive
twirl-leap!

If Luna can pass the exam she'll be a real dancer.
Luna is next...

Double. Tap. Spin.
Duck. Dive.
Trip! Fall!

She gets up,
takes a moment
and tries again...

Double. Tap. Spin.
Duck. Dive.
Trip. Fall.

She tries again.
Double. Tap. Spin.
Trip. Stumble. Fall!
Ouch!

Luna watches from the floor
as most of the class:
double-tap-spin, duck-dive, twirl-leap!

Watches as most of the class pass the exam.
Watches as most of the class become real dancers.

And it's like all sounds have been muffled,
like all colours have been dulled.
Like sunlight has been snatched away
from behind every cloud.

Mum and Dad tell her, "It's ok, not to worry.
Practice makes perfect. You can still dance."
"But I'll never be a real dancer," says Luna.

Mum takes Luna to see a musical.
Dancers leap and bound, tap and spin,
under golden lights. During the interval
Luna shimmies to the ice cream seller.
It's like all colours are starting to glow a little.

"See, you're dancing!" says Mum.
"But I'll never be a real dancer," says Luna.

At Grandpa and Nana's house Luna plays their old jazz records and together they do dance moves called the Crazy Legs, Charleston and Heels, strutting and laughing. It feels like all the colours are starting to sparkle a little.

"See, you're dancing," says Nana.
"But I'll never be a real dancer," says Luna.

Dad takes Luna to Carnival where she dances
in the crowd to the booming bass
and swirling tunes.

She does dance moves like the Rockaway and the Scooby Doo,
ducking and diving, twirling and smiling.

"See, you're dancing!" says Dad.
"But I'll never be a real dancer," says Luna.

Dad lifts Luna up...

"A sun is a star when it shines,
a bell is a chime when it rings.
You're a real dancer when you dance
and your moves make colours sing."

Luna is at her cousin's birthday party.
After the candles are blown out
and the cake is eaten,
everyone plays games.

And then Grandpa puts
the music on and Luna's song
comes on and a space is cleared.
So she...

double-tap-spins,
duck-dives,
twirls and LEAPS!

Leaps like she has never leapt before
soaring high, like she is flying.

And everyone gasps and says...
"Luna you are a real dancer!"

And it's like the world's volume has been turned up, as Luna teaches her friends to shimmy.

Like all the colours are tapping their feet, as Luna shows Dad how to pirouette.

Like the sun is boogieing behind every cloud, as Luna and Mum do the Crazy Legs!

As Nana and Grandpa Rockaway and spin.
As Luna shows everyone
how to leap, leap, leap over hard times,
with joy bounding
in your heart.

Luna loves dance.